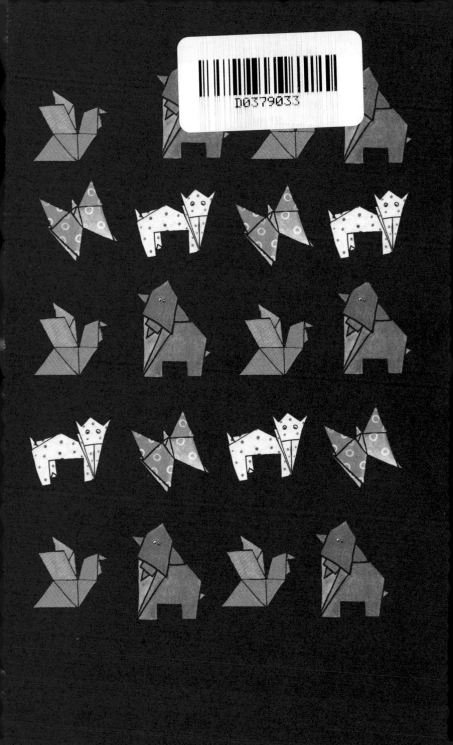

CHOP-CHOP, MAD CAP!

JULIETTE SAUMANDE

ILLUSTRATED BY SADIE CRAMER

CHOP-CHOP, MAD CAP!
Published 2012
by Little Island
7 Kenilworth Park
Dublin 6W
Ireland

www.littleisland.ie

ISBN 978-1-908195-21-0

Design by Paul Woods | www.paulthedesigner.ie

Printed in Poland by Drukarnia Skleniarz

Little Island received financial assistance from
The Arts Council (An Chomhairle Ealaíon), Dublin, Ireland.

10 9 8 7 6 5 4 3

To the two AO'Cs
May they be super
May they be fun
May they eat their veg
(Not necessarily in that order)

ABOUT THE ILLUSTRATOR

Sadie Cramer, from Teignmouth, Devon, studied Fine Art Sculpture at the University of Ulster in Belfast. After graduating in 1993, she moved to London, where she worked in art departments for film and television. For the past 16 years she has lived in a top secret hideout on the shores of Lough Corrib near Galway with her husband, Mark Hand, and their four children. Much of her work involves teaching and coordinating children's art projects. Sadie loves singing opera very loudly, a good story and the colour pink.

ABOUT THE AUTHOR

Juliette Saumande is French. That means:

- she knows two hundred and thirty-one words for 'cheese' (and a few more for 'smelly')
- she speaks French to her two cats (though they usually pretend to only understand English) and
- she believes warm summers are for real, somewhere.

Now, though, she lives in Dublin where she has learned:

- two hundred and thirty-one words for 'rain'
- the art of climbing on the top deck of the 40 bus and
- the delights of toasted sandwiches.

She's written lots of picture books in French and she has also translated novels for young and younger people. She has a website (www.juliettesaumande.com) and a blog (www.juliettesaumande.blogspot.com). Juliette lives with her better, more bearded half and her Best Boy and Girl. She loves liquorice, but she thinks Crunchies should be banned and their recipe thrown into a bottomless pit. She wishes you a good day.

THANKING YE

Right, this is going to be a bit long so have a good old stretch now, a wee yawn if you need it, and I can begin.*

Alternatively, you can just skip this bit and go straight to the story. But you never know, you might just have made it to the acknowledgements. Wouldn't it be a pity to miss YOUR NAME in print? Mmmh?

Here goes:

- First of all, and as promised, this one is for Sorcha Mellon-Whelan and the girls from way back when in St. Raphaela's Primary School, Stillorgan (although they've probably all grown beards by now).
- Nat for all the time reading aloud and all the allowed reading time (and for the meringues).
- The Best Boy and the French Lady, just because.
- The Best of Natives on the Little Island, Siobhán and Elaina, for allowing me to camp with them.
- The crowd at Children's Books Ireland for providing the most excellent company, great laughs and inspiration opportunities.
- Pauline, Paddy, Ger and the lasses on the writing group for laughing at my jokes, liking my biscuits and believing in Mad Cap.
- The staff, cook and landscape at Tyrone Guthrie Centre at Annaghmakerrig. The final draft of this book and my extra kilos number 7 and 8 thank you kindly.
- Jane Austen for inspiration (kind of).
- And finally, You, Dear Reader. Didn't I say you'd be in there somewhere?

RENT-A-HERO!
FAST, STRONG, RELIABLE, AMAZING

MAD CAP

SOLVES ALL YOUR PROBLEMS AND MYSTERIES

MISSING CATS, TRICKY MATHS
BIG BULLIES, MUSHY PEAS ...
YOU NAME IT, SHE'S ONTO IT!

1

MIDNIGHT RAID

The bedroom was darker than the old loo in the back garden, and Madgie M. Cappock, aka Mad Cap, stood there waiting for her eyes to adjust and scratching her nose furiously. She was wearing her superhero cape (which was great for camouflage) and her superhero mask (which was dreadful for itchy noses).

The bedroom belonged to her big brother Colm and she could hear him snoring like a cat with asthma. But that didn't worry Madgie. It was all part of The Plan, the plan her best friend

Norbert Soup had carefully designed. Norbert was officially a genius and Madgie knew she could count on his brilliant brains to get her out of impossible situations as well as into them.

Just like tonight. Tonight, Mad Cap's mission was to uncover a potentially juicy secret: the name of her brother's girlfriend. And for that she needed Colm's diary. And for that she needed to sneak into his bedroom in the dead of night.

She could see a bit better now: the outline of the Captain Gut posters on the wall, Colm's trainee chef gear neatly stashed in a corner … Madgie licked her lips in the darkness at the thought of the delish dessert he'd baked that very evening. But she had to stay focused. This was an important mission – vital even. This was going to prove that the Rent-a-Hero agency she and Norbert had recently put together could handle tricky, perhaps dangerous, operations. If they could pull this one off, they would know for sure that they were ready to advertise their services (outside of school and their own family circles) as general finders-out and useful superheroes.

After all, there was only so much fun you could have tracking down misplaced plastic buckets in playgrounds or following around odd-looking teachers to make sure they were not zombies in disguise.

No, Mad Cap couldn't afford to mess this up.

As she tiptoed across the room, Colm suddenly lashed out an arm in his sleep and caught a handful of her cape.

This was *not* part of The Plan. Madgie panicked. She stepped away from Colm's bed, but his grip was firm and he didn't let go. Worse, he gave a big yawn and started burbling. Madgie froze. What was she supposed to do? She tried to remember Norbert's Plan:

One: Get in

Two: Get it

Three: Get out

She repeated The Plan over and over until she had calmed down. Then she tugged gently at her cape and prised it out of Colm's fist. She wasn't a superhero for nothing.

Mad Cap forever and beyond! she thought triumphantly.

But maybe she was thinking too loudly, because just then Colm grabbed her by the hand and began to mumble something. It sounded like 'sitting in a tree' …

Mad Cap pricked up her ears. She couldn't believe it. He was singing in his sleep! This was too good. If he kept this up, she wouldn't need to find his stupid diary at all. He'd just sing out the name she was after.

But then Colm began to *spell*. 'K-I-S … K-I-S-I-N-G …'

Madgie snorted. Even *she* was a better speller than that. But now Colm was squeezing her hand and – yuk! – kissing it!

Come on! she thought to him. *Sing! Who's sitting in that rotten tree with you?*

But Colm was snoring again now.

With a quiet sigh, Madgie wriggled her hand free of his. It was time for part 2 of The Plan: *Get it*.

Her eyes had almost adjusted to the darkness by now. Almost. She bumped her knee against the bedside locker.

'Janie!' she muttered. 'That *hurt*!'

She rubbed at her knee. Then she remembered she'd been eating chocolate buttons. And she was wearing new pyjamas under her superhero cape. *Mum'll kill me!*

Then Colm started sleep-singing again, and Mad Cap thought he might kill her too if he woke up and found her in his room. *Better get a move on.*

She opened the locker and a pile of smelly underwear tumbled out. She rummaged in it. First she found a couple of battered comic books. Then came a cracked tennis ball and a soft rabbit that felt suspiciously like one she had lost years ago. At last, she found what she had been looking for: Colm's secret diary.

She went to the window to signal SUCCESS to Norbert, who was (in theory) watching from his own bedroom on the other side of the street. Madgie slipped behind the curtains and took out her mini torch. She paused. She had to get this right. What had Norbert said? Two flashes for 'OK' and one for 'hard luck'. Or was it the other way round? She knew she should check – Norbert had written it all down for her on a

piece of paper – but she couldn't be bothered. She just wanted to get out of there as soon as possible. The Captain Gut posters on the walls looked like they were about to come alive and Colm could wake up at any moment.

I'll flash three times, she decided. *Norbert will understand. He's a genius, after all.*

She turned the torch on and off, and again, and again, always taking care to aim at Norbert's house across the street.

Then she waited for his reply.

Nothing.

Maybe he had fallen asleep? In fairness, it was gone midnight, she realised with a yawn.

She signalled again.

Still no reply.

This was getting *boring*.

Then she remembered that she had Colm's diary in her hot and chocolatey fist. She knew she wasn't supposed to open it before she met up with Norbert again. But Mad Cap couldn't wait. She decided she really wanted to know now. Really, really. And anyway, *where* was Norbert?

She looked out the window. Still nothing. Behind her, Colm was now imitating a French horn. Quite convincingly, too.

Mad Cap scratched her nose again and opened the diary. She shone the torch on it. It was full of concert tickets, old photos, bus timetables, phone numbers and, every now and then, a few spidery words that she couldn't make out.

Does he write with his toes or what?!

She thought of the cookbook Colm kept in a glass case down in the kitchen, with its pristine cloth cover and neatly copied recipes. She wondered if her brother used a clone every time he was on dinner duty. No matter how you looked at it, Colm was a mystery. With a sigh, Madgie shut the diary again. She wouldn't find out tonight, then. Oh, well.

She glanced into the street. She would count to ten, she decided. If Norbert hadn't replied by then, she'd go to bed.

She had reached eight when she noticed a flickering white light on the other side of the street. At first she thought it was Norbert answering her at last, but then she realised the light wasn't coming from Norbert's house. It was coming from the house next door to his.

Who lives there? she tried to remember. (Well, it was very late.) *And who lives there who would be signalling with a torch to ME in the middle of the night?*

The light kept on flickering. Whoever it was must be desperate to make contact.

The Fitzmarcels, she suddenly remembered. They were new people. They'd opened a butcher's shop just in the last week or two. And apparently they liked sending weird signals across the street in the night. Or … could Norbert have gone next door for some reason and was now trying to attract her attention?

Well, she couldn't very well go and knock on the butcher's door and ask if they were holding Norbert hostage or something. Whatever was going on, it would have to wait till the morning.

She turned from the window, promptly tripped over her brother's chaos and banged into the bed. Colm woke up with a start. He grabbed her hand and spluttered, 'What are you doing here?' and 'Yurgh! Is that chocolate?'

This time, Mad Cap was ready. Section B29(f) of Norbert's Plan (the long version) popped into her head and she knew what she had to do. She shook free of her brother's grip and said, 'You're dreaming, Colm. It's just a dream.'

For a second he stared at her as if she had three heads, then he fell back on his pillow. In an instant he was snoring again, but Mad Cap was already gone.

MORNING ROW

Next morning, Madgie woke up with a headache. It was as if somebody was playing a Rocky film inside her head. *Punch, punch, punch.* When her brain cleared a bit, she realised the punching was actually coming from the box-room.

'Oh no,' she moaned as she copped what was going on. 'I have boxing practice with Dad today!'

Mr Cappock, Madgie's dad, was a guard. His mum was a guard and his great-uncle was a guard, and there was nothing he wanted more than to pass the gift on to the next generation.

Colm was a hopeless case, being a trainee chef and a rebel, but there was still Madgie. Hence the boxing practice on Saturday mornings, the watching of *Law and Order* on Sundays and the 'friendly wrestling' over the remote every other night.

Usually Madgie didn't mind the routine, as she managed to get the better of Dad by using unconventional weapons like tickling and shrieking at the top of her voice. But this morning, she had no time for it. She had to go to Norbert's to report the mission's success and she had to find out about Colm's girlfriend. But first she HAD to get breakfast.

She rushed to the kitchen, scoffed down a scone and some juice and ran out the door. She was halfway through the front garden before she realised she was still in her pyjamas.

Never mind, she thought. *No one'll notice, if I'm quick enough.*

'Nice outfit!' a voice called out.

Madgie stopped dead. Her mum was at the living-room window, looking flushed and tired, but not in a grumpy sort of way. In fact, she was smiling. Madgie relaxed.

'What are you up to, bean?' Mrs Cappock continued. 'Off to Norbert's to right some wrong, young hero?'

Madgie frowned. What was Mum talking about? What did she *know*?

It was like Mrs Cappock had a seventh sense: she always knew when there was some sort of mischief about. (Her sixth sense she used to find anything anybody in the family had ever lost around the house, from car keys to botched homework to good manners.)

'Come on in,' Mum said again. 'I've got a mission for you.'

Madgie's guilt and fear lifted for a moment. A mission? That'd be good – *really* good. The Rent-a-Hero agency could do with some real business and some real money coming in. There was this deadly pair of superhero boots Madgie had seen in the shop only the other day, with side pockets and a secret compartment built into the heel. Just what she needed to hide her snacks in.

But then she remembered she was talking to her mother and that they probably had very different definitions of the word 'mission'.

She ran back into the house and zoomed up to her room to grab a hoodie. At least it would hide some of the chocolate stains, and she could stuff Colm's diary in the front pocket. Come to think of it, she could stash a few cereal bars in there, too.

She darted down to the living-room and plonked herself on a beanbag. Mrs Cappock frowned, noticing the strange bulge in Madgie's front pocket, but then she started to rub something away behind her glasses. Surely it couldn't be tears? Maybe she had something in her eye. But there was no time to investigate because, just then, an almighty roar sprang from Colm's bedroom, flooded the landing and crashed down the stairs.

Before the yelling tsunami had time to reach the living-room, Mad Cap had pressed her hands deep down into her hoodie pocket and made a run for it.

Even from Norbert's doorstep, she could still hear her brother bawling across the road. She couldn't be sure, of course, but she thought it went something like, 'WHO'S THE NASTY GNOME THAT STOLE MY DIARY?'

Norbert Soup opened the door even before Mad Cap knocked. His hair was sticking out as if he'd been electrocuted, and he looked particularly grumpy.

'We'd better get out of here' he said, closing the door behind him. 'My sisters are watching a replay of *University Challenge*. They support different teams. It could turn nasty.'

As they made their way to their hiding place under the Grand Canal Bridge, Madgie noticed that her friend was carrying a small leather suitcase. She also noticed that he wasn't saying anything about the strange midnight goings on that nearly wrecked their plan, so eventually she spluttered: 'What happened to you last night? Did you fall asleep in front of *Countdown* or what?'

Understanding Mad Cap as she spoke through a mouthful of cereal bars was one of Norbert's fortes.

'No', he said with a scowl. 'I got caught under Scrum. He sat on me all night. I couldn't move. Happy?'

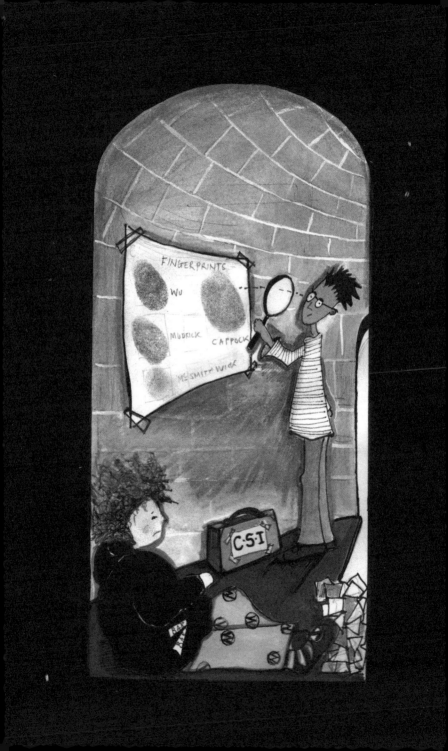

Scrum was the Soups' cat. It was probably the most enormous cat you've ever seen. If you met him in the dark, you might mistake him for a small elephant. Mad Cap had been stuck under him once and she knew for a fact that Norbert was telling the truth. Still, there was no need to be rude.

She handed him the diary and waited.

'OK,' he said, opening the suitcase. 'We want to do this properly. One, fingerprint analysis. Two, dating of paper. Three, graphology.'

Madgie rolled her eyes. What was he talking about? At this rate, Colm would be married and they still wouldn't know the stupid name! But Norbert was very strict on these things and there was nothing she could do.

So while he examined the cover with a magnifying glass and a home-made chart containing the fingerprints of the people living on Barnaby Street, she sat back and tried to fold her cereal bar wrapper into a frog shape. She remembered the instructions from her *Origami for Beginners* book, but the wrapper wasn't behaving and she was getting nowhere.

Normally, she liked origami because it was totally foolproof. Once you knew what valleys and mountains were and so long as you followed the simple guidelines, you could make some really cool stuff really easily. But right now, it just wouldn't work.

Madgie made a grumpy crumple of her wrapper and looked at Norbert. He was still bending over the diary, turning the pages slowly, slowly. Behind the magnifying glass, his eyes looked like two gigantic chocolate buttons going back and forth on the page, back and forth, back … Madgie felt herself nodding off.

'I see!' Norbert snapped finally.

Madgie started. She had been half-dozing, thinking about Mum's funny face earlier and wondering if there really *had* been tears behind her glasses. Maybe it was just dust. Or onions.

'What?'

Norbert looked at her sternly.

'I'll give you the full result of my investigation when I'm finished.'

With that, he fished a little bottle of clear liquid out of the suitcase. Only then did Madgie notice the sticker on the case: Barnaby Street CSI Kit™, N. Soup Designer.

'What's CSI again?' she asked, startling Norbert, who sent the bottle crashing to the ground. 'Sorry.'

He gave her a nasty look.

'It stands for Crime Scene Investigation,' he replied curtly. 'Now if you don't mind, I have work to do.'

And he turned his back on her.

Soon Madgie was bored out of her mind. She was also getting very cross. After all, *she* had done all the dangerous work while Norbert was safely in bed with his fat cat. So why couldn't she do the scientific stuff, too? True, the Rent-a-Hero thing had been Norbert's idea and he was the genius on the team, but *she* was the hero for rent – *she* had the outfit!

She was about to give Norbert a piece of her mind when he turned round again and handed her a sheet of paper.

'If you ever have any information that's

actually interesting,' he hissed, 'please let me know.'

He packed the case and got up.

'Otherwise,' he added as he walked away, 'don't bother.'

Madgie was dumbstruck. What had happened? She looked at the sheet.

REPORT
Results of the examination of Colm Cappock's secret diary (exhibit A) as held on Saturday the 12th under the Grand Canal Bridge as carefully as possible considering the presence of Some People.

Some people? Mad Cap thought. *Who's that? There was only me!*

1/ FINGERPRINT ANALYSIS:

Many prints found both on cover and inside pages. Compared to the Potential Suspects and Witnesses File (area of Barnaby Street). All the fingerprints belong to same person: Madgie M. Cappock.

2/ DATING OF PAPER:

Examination interrupted due to wreckage of bottle containing the revealing agent.

3/ GRAPHOLOGY:

Examination rendered impossible by the GAZILLION CHOCOLATE STAINS ALL OVER THE PLACE.

'What? What? There weren't that many, I'm sure.'

CONCLUSION:
I'm sick of this. Useless clues, useless exhibits, USELESS PARTNER!
I QUIT!!

A RIGHT RIOT

Madgie sat under the Grand Canal Bridge, completely alone and totally flummoxed. Her best pal had just walked out on her for no good reason that she could see. He had also taken away Colm's secret diary, and with it Madgie's last hope of peace at home.

And what about Rent-a-Hero? Was it all over before it had even properly begun? No more missions?

This reminded her of her mum. Hadn't she said something about a mission this morning, before Colm started squealing the house down?

Madgie decided to find out. Then she would do whatever it was on her own, without telling Norbert, and he would be impressed when she was able to report back to him about her success. And then they could be friends again.

While she thought this over, she had another go at that frog origami pattern. This time the paper was doing what it was supposed to do and her fingers worked automatically without the assistance of her brain.

Finally, she made her way home, wondering what she should charge her mother for doing this mission. A new origami book? A whole month without tidying duties? No mushy peas for a year?

She was so caught up in thought that she didn't see Colm storming out of the front door as she came through the gate.

'You!' he said in a cold, hard voice. 'Empty your pockets. Now!'

For a minute, Mad Cap just stared at the icy face of Captain Gut on her brother's T-shirt. She gulped and looked up. Just now, Colm was the spitting image of the comic book villain: white as a sheet, with clenched jaws and a give-no-quarters kind of look in his eyes.

'Your pockets, I said!' he repeated, grabbing her by the wrist.

She knew she couldn't wriggle out of this one, so she complied. Out came two cereal bar wrappers, one elastic band, a piece of paper folded in the shape of a frog and a handful of fluff.

'I'm sure you have it!' Colm raged as he stomped off. 'If it's not in your room or in your pockets, it must be in that secret place of yours down by the canal. I'll find it!'

Madgie waited until he was well away from the house before sighing a tiny sigh of relief. At least some good had come of her falling-out with Norbert. If he hadn't taken the diary with him, she would have been caught red-handed and that would have been the end of Mad Cap.

She gently stroked the origami frog. If you looked at it carefully, you could just about make out some writing:

Results of the examination of

Madgie put the frog gingerly back into her pocket.

'Mad Cap for ever and beyond!' she whispered as she went into the house.

But as soon as she was past the door, she felt worried again. What had Colm said? 'If it's not in your room ...' *How did he know that?* she wondered. She ran upstairs to see what damage her brother had done to her bedroom and what else he might have discovered in there.

'Bean!'

Madgie stopped halfway up the stairs. Her mother's timing was terrible. What did she want this time?

'*Beeeean!*'

Madgie could tell by Mum's tone that her room would have to wait. She trotted back downstairs again and out to the back garden.

Mrs Cappock was rummaging in her tool box. She took out a trowel and threw it back into the shed before picking up a tiny rake that was lying in the grass and dropping it into the box. She closed it with a clunk and turned around.

Madgie looked at her closely. If there had been anything wrong with Mum earlier, she seemed to be grand now. She was wearing her brand new red and tan gloves, her work dungarees and her gardening apron, the beige one with all the pockets, but it was tied in a funny way around her waist, as if it had shrunk in the wash. Madgie suddenly remembered that pack of lemon sherbet she had forgotten in her jeans pocket last week. Her trousers had come out of the machine looking a bit yellow and … fizzy. Surely that wasn't why Mum's apron looked odd, was it?

27

'Madgie,' her mum said, hauling her heavy case up onto a wheelbarrow. 'I'm off to sort out Miss Wu's hedge and then to see what I can do about the ant invasion in the playground. Could you do me a favour and pop into the butcher's for some mince?'

The butcher's! Mad Cap suddenly remembered the flickering light from the Fitzmarcels' shop the night before.

So *that* was Mum's mission for her. To go shopping for mince. *Way* below Mad Cap's abilities, Madgie thought. But still. She was a hero and heroes are here to help those who need it.

But mince? That sounded suspicious. There was only one person in her family who truly liked mince. And it was not a person Madgie truly liked.

'Could I get rashers instead, Mum?'

'No, sweetpea, Grandma's coming to dinner and her new teeth haven't arrived yet.'

Grandma. *Perfect.* Not exactly Madgie's favourite person.

As Madgie dragged her misery and crushed

hopes up the driveway, she heard her mum calling out again, 'Look on the bright side, young hero. You can keep the change!'

Madgie grumbled to herself, wondering what was the hardest mince she could possibly get, as she walked the few yards to Mr Fitzmarcel's butcher shop.

There was a huge queue of ancient ladies, all come to buy their kitties' breakfasts. Mr Fitzmarcel was new and quite a talking point with the neighbours, though Mad Cap couldn't see why he was so interesting. He was just a boring, fat butcher. (Who signalled across the street in the middle of the night ... Hmm.)

She sighed. What a waste of Rent-a-Hero's time! Seriously, anybody could do it and the chances of a giant hairy monster jumping onto a crowded pavement were pretty slim. Boring. *Boring.* BORING.

The lady in front of Madgie in the queue turned round and gave her a sour look. It was Mrs Mudrick, the meanest old thing on Barnaby Street. She lived next door to the butcher, on the other side from Norbert. She hissed at Mad Cap

for no earthly reason and turned around again.

Madgie stuck her tongue out at her – behind her back of course – and noticed that Mrs Mudrick seemed to have mistaken a bottle of Ribena for her shampoo. Again. She wondered why the oldies never had white hair, always purple or blue.

As she waited, Madgie thought about the flashing light once more. Had it really come from the shop last night? Or had it just been the headlights of some car on the street? Maybe she could ask Mr Fitzmarcel, she thought, and use this silly mission to investigate a proper mystery.

The queue moved slowly as the women commented on the weather, the butcher shouted to his apprentice and a man came to ask could he put up his posters in the window please, thanks very much.

'Easy, laddie,' Mr Fitzmarcel said, although the man had grey hair coming out of his ears and nose and could have been the butcher's great-uncle. 'What are the posters for?'

The older man beamed. 'The Barnaby Street panto!' he said to the delight of the grannies. 'It's called *Tap! Tap! Tap!* It's got tap dancing in it. And rabbits. And plumbers. And …'

By now, the butcher was glaring at him and stroking his big knife menacingly.

'Do I look like I want to support tap-dancing rabbits?' he bellowed. 'And *she's* a plumber,' he roared, pointing at a beefy woman near the back door. 'So I've got enough of those, too. Now get out of my shop!'

Mr Fitzmarcel wasn't exactly meek, as the old ladies had discovered since he'd arrived in Barnaby Street, but this was the first time they'd seen him actually threaten anybody, and for such a simple request, too. The women muttered their disapproval behind their shopping bags and Madgie made a mental note never to ask the butcher to put up ads for Rent-a-Hero. They could do with the publicity, but Madgie didn't want to annoy an already angry man with a big knife.

Madgie thought she was going to die of starvation and boredom in front of the pork chops counter when, at last, it was Mrs Mudrick's turn.

'Now, *laddie*,' she said pointedly, 'I'm here for

a nice bit of steak for my little Sapphire. I want the best, of course, not last week's offal like you give every body else.'

Madgie could see the butcher's face turning the colour of his apron: very pale from the top of his bald head to his chin, with a scary streak of red across his nose and cheeks.

'I don't want old meat,' Mrs Mudrick concluded.

Mr Fitzmarcel forced himself to put the knife down and took a deep, long breath.

Obviously too long for Mrs M's taste, who lifted her chin and squared her shoulders before adding: 'Hurry now laddie. Chop-chop!'

The butcher leaned over the counter.

'Chop-chop is right' he snarled, picking up his knife again. 'Listen to me, the only *old* thing in this shop is its customers! Now get out of here, you lot!' he shouted coming into the queue and shooing people out. 'We're closed for the day!'

He banged the door shut and stomped back into the depths of the shop.

Had he come out, he would have noticed a crooked poster only inches away from his door that said:

Madgie, on the other hand, saw it quite well, this poster, as the crowd of old women pressed her against it. There was a picture of a yellow rabbit wearing a top hat. It was so awful she could have drawn it herself.

'Can't you see you're in my way?' came a creaky, mean old voice.

It was Mrs Mudrick. Madgie wasn't anything like in her way, but she said nothing. The woman had vengeance written all over her face, so when she walked over to Mad Cap, the girl instinctively stepped back.

'Listen,' Mrs Mudrick growled, 'I'm aware you're a useless child and up to no good and, knowing what I know, I can only pity your poor mother. But I don't have a choice. Since the shop opened, my Sapphire only eats meat from this ...' – here she said a rude word that was fashionable when she was born and dinosaurs roamed the plains of Ireland – 'of a butcher.'

She stuffed two grubby coins into Madgie's hand.

'Your mother tells me you're looking for a job of some sort. Well, as soon as he reopens,' she said, 'and, you hear me, not a second later, I want you to get a nice juicy steak and bring it to my house. You'll do this for me every day. Understood?'

Mad Cap was gobsmacked and, come to think of it, not very pleased. Were all her missions going to involve shopping for meat? And what was that about her 'poor mother'? Did Manic Mudrick know something Madgie didn't?

As Mrs Mudrick hobbled away, laughing her rollers off, Madgie thought for a second that she could hear some crazy music like in the films when the madwoman stabs people in the loo. Or was it in the shower? But it must have been her imagination. Surely?

ALIENS AND DONKEY SAUSAGE

Life became very funny for Madgie over the next few days.

Mum decided to clear the house of what she called 'junk food', from fizzy drinks to stinky cheeses, chicken pâté (no loss there) and Jaffa cakes. She kept falling asleep when Mad Cap told her about her day at school and, once, she said she was too tired to do her usual rounds of the neighbourhood gardens. Madgie was quite shocked, but not as shocked as when Mum told her to be a pet and ring Grandma and ask if she could come and stay for a while. (Strangely, when Madgie tried to ring her grandmother, she never could get through …)

Meanwhile, Norbert was trying his best to avoid her and, since he was a genius, he was succeeding. She caught a glimpse of him at school one day when she went into the boys' changing room. But that was by mistake and all she saw were his socks. They were furry and had a little pompom stuck on the back of each heel. Then about a dozen boys noticed her standing in the doorway and she'd had to retreat under the attack of smelly T-shirts and sweaty runners.

As if all this wasn't bad enough, Colm was forever accusing her of having stolen his diary and thrown it into the canal. On Tuesday, he had started a protest strike and announced he wouldn't cook so much as banana on toast until he got his diary back.

There was nothing Mad Cap could do about that, since Norbert still had it, but she couldn't explain this to Colm.

As a result of all that, Madgie spent a lot of time on her own, folding her way through *Origami for Beginners*. That wasn't so bad. But as soon as she closed her book and left her paper shapes behind, her brain leaped back to the same question over and over again: *How come everything's gone so wrong?*

She felt strange and out of kilter. And that worried her.

The worst of it all, though, was the business with Mrs Mudrick. On the first day of her new mission, as soon as Mr Fitzmarcel had reopened, Mad Cap had gone back to the butcher's for Sapphire's meat.

Only it wasn't Mr Fitzmarcel. Maybe he was still sulking at the back of the shop? Anyway, it was *Mrs* Fitzmarcel, the plumber lady, who was serving now, and she couldn't tell the difference between a chop and a chicken. She had given Madgie something that looked suspiciously like black pudding, insisting it was what Sapphire usually ate.

'And *what* is that?' Mrs Mudrick had raged when Madgie brought her the meat. 'Donkey sausage?'

Mad Cap swallowed. Donkey sausage? What kind of a monster did you have to be to even *think* of turning donkeys into sausages? She had fled the old woman's house as if an axe murderer was after her.

It had taken some guts to go back there the next morning. But she had done it. She wasn't a superhero for nothing.

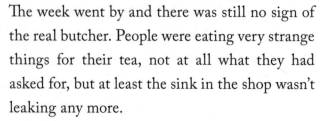

The week went by and there was still no sign of the real butcher. People were eating very strange things for their tea, not at all what they had asked for, but at least the sink in the shop wasn't leaking any more.

Every night, Madgie tried to make contact with Norbert from the bathroom window with her torch. He did signal back all right, but it was such a flurry of flashes that Madgie could only conclude that he was probably saying 'eat your shoes'. This would have been typical Norbert on a grumpy day.

She saw the strange white lights flashing from the butcher's shop a few times too and still could make nothing of them.

By Thursday, the batteries of her torch had died. A whole zoo of paper animals had taken over her bedroom. And people on Barnaby Street were starting to think that Mr Fitzmarcel had been abducted by aliens. Or maybe Mrs Fitzmarcel had clobbered him with a drainpipe. (And maybe he had deserved it.)

On Friday, Mad Cap found a note stuck with ancient Blu-tack to Mrs Mudrick's door when she came by with Sapphire's meat.

GONE TO THE HOSPITAL TO ANNOY A SICK NEIGHBOUR.

- BRING THE STEAK INTO THE KITCHEN. DOOR IS OPEN.

- DO NOT TOUCH ANYTHING IN THE HOUSE.

PS: TO ANYONE WHO ISN'T MADGIE C., DON'T EVEN DREAM OF GOING IN. SAPPHIRE WILL TEAR YOU TO SHREDS.

Mad Cap shuddered. She hadn't actually met Sapphire yet. She had only seen her huge, mean eyes glinting in the dark corridor behind Mrs Mudrick's legs when Madgie had come to deliver the meat over the past few days.

But she had heard the terrifying squeals when Sapphire took on other cats. It sounded like a banshee with a sore throat. Sapphire once had a go at Norbert's cat, Scrum. That's when Scrum had decided to become a cat hermit, as Norbert put it: Scrum now stayed inside, eating his way to becoming a small elephant.

Turning the doorknob hesitantly, Madgie wondered if she was doing the right thing. Should she come back later? Should she come back *armed*? How would Sapphire know it was her and not some unwanted intruder? What would stop the evil beast throwing herself at Mad Cap's throat? And what in the name of God was that foul smell?!

The door opened slowly into a Black Pit of Doom which, as soon as Madgie found the light switch, turned into a narrow corridor with flowery wallpaper that was so old, the roses on it looked as if they had actually withered. The same pattern was repeated on the horrible lino that covered the floor, except for a bluish blob further down.

A blob that was hissing and growling and was very possibly called Sapphire.

Mad Cap took a deep breath. Holding the bag from the butcher's in front of her like a shield, she started towards the cat, who seemed to be guarding one of the two doors on either side of the corridor.

'Here, kitty, kitty,' she faltered, thinking that these weren't great Famous Last Words for a superhero.

Sapphire took a step towards Mad Cap and her growl deepened.

Madgie wished Mrs Mudrick's neighbour hadn't had to go to hospital and that Mrs Mudrick didn't have to go and annoy her and that … oh, *anything* rather than be here with this *beast*.

She could see Sapphire's teeth very clearly now and for a second she knew exactly what was going to happen next. It involved a jumping fury and lots and lots of bite marks.

She stayed where she was, with her back to the door and her feet leaving dirty prints on the ugly lino. Her hands, her chest, her whole body felt as if it had been taken over by an army of angry ants that marched under her skin, making it impossible to move and painful to breathe.

She had to do something. She had to think. And fast. But her mind was reaching panic mode as the spitting cat kept coming. She thought about Norbert. If only she were a genius, too!

She groped frantically in her brain for anything that could be useful. *Come on!* She had faced danger before. Raiding her brother's bedroom at midnight was no joke! She vaguely remembered how she had panicked when Colm had grabbed her arm in his sleep. But she'd had Norbert and his brilliant plans to guide her at the time. To save her. 'One: do this. Two: do that. Three …'

But now she was on her own, with no one to say 'One, two, three' for her.

Sapphire was halfway up the corridor, growling louder than a boy-racer car zooming down the road. Madgie's heart was beating fast and loud, like a pair of crazy castanets.

One, two, three, she thought. *One, two, three.*

And suddenly it was as if Norbert were there, talking to her, telling her what to do. Or rather, *how* to do. She had to make her own plan. She had to stare her problem in the face and chop it up like Mr Fitzmarcel used to carve up meat.

'One: open the kitchen door,' she murmured, feeling her heart slowing down. 'Two: throw in the food.'

She realised she could shake her legs and her arms. The angry ants weren't so angry anymore.

'Three: make a run for it.'

She was back to herself now. She could breathe. She could move. And she could see that, as plans went, it wasn't terribly refined, but it would have to do.

Sapphire stayed put, her eyes like headlights on the paper bag. Madgie had reached the first door. The smell in the hall reminded her of the spray Mum used to 'decontaminate' the loo, and also of Grandma's perfume. She opened the door, hoping that it was the kitchen and that the stench wouldn't be so bad in there.

It was a living-room. At least, it was a room with a big armchair and a telly. The rest was completely taken over by knitting stuff: there were needles in the vases, balls of wool in the fruit bowl, piles of pink and blue baby cardies and, spread on the coffee table, a massive square thing, maybe a blanket, all red and black.

So much for part one of her plan.

Madgie went up to the table. OK, she wasn't supposed to be in this room at all, but Mrs Mudrick's note hadn't said anything about looking, had it? As long as she didn't *touch* anything, she was grand.

All around the edges of the blanket – which she could see now wasn't finished – were big black knives with a red tip, all so neatly knitted that you might have thought they were real. In each corner was a black skull with red eyes and in the middle of the piece were just two words. Two words that were enough to make Madgie run out of the room, skid on the lino as far as the second door in the corridor, trip over a furious Sapphire and tumble into the kitchen.

She unwrapped the butcher's parcel and dumped it in the cat's plate without even realising it wasn't meat at all but a white, 100% veggie tofu steak. She bumped into Sapphire again, threw the bag in an overflowing bin and rushed to the front door.

It was only later, at home, after tea and a bath and some 'friendly wrestling', that she allowed herself to think about what she had seen on Mrs Mudrick's coffee table. She took out her superhero's secret mission log and copied it down:

FITZMARCEL DIE!

THE TEMPLE OF CODES

On Saturday morning, Mad Cap came to a decision. She had to talk to Norbert, no matter what. There was a missing man, a potential butcher-killer on the loose and a history essay she needed to finish for Monday.

She wrote out in her log book everything she had discovered so far. She made it as neat as possible, with drawings and stuff, so that her

friend would be impressed – which he would have been if she hadn't left the notebook on the kitchen table as she grabbed an oatmeal muffin before setting out for the Soups' house.

She was already crossing the road when she realised this. She would have had time to go back and get it, but she was simply too dumbstruck by what she had just seen.

And that was a rabbit.

Now, rabbits are common animals. But not *this* rabbit. It was ginormous, it was furry, it was bright yellow and it was Norbert.

Madgie forced herself to move. She approached cautiously, bending double, keeping the little dishevelled hedge between herself and the beast. She noticed something else now. People were queuing outside her friend's house. They would walk up to a table where Mrs Soup was seated with a neat notepad and perfectly sharpened pencils. Then they would stare at the big yellow fluffy thing, laugh like maniacs and sign Mrs Soup's book.

What was going on?

'Are you in yet?'

The voice made Madgie jump. She turned around. It was the old man who had put up the posters for the panto.

'They'll be looking for young'uns like yourself.'

She looked at him blankly.

'It's gonna be a good show,' he added. 'The best bit of tap dancing in a long time, I'm told.'

He tipped his cap and tapped his way away. Then, at long last, the penny dropped. *Tap! Tap! Tap!* The Soups were enrolling people for the panto auditions!

Mad Cap didn't fancy tap dancing all that much, but she thought pretending to want to enter the audition would be a good excuse to talk to Norbert.

She took a deep breath and approached the rabbit and his mum.

'Ah, Madgie!' cried Mrs Soup. 'How's your poor dear mother? Do you want to sign up or are you here to see Norbert?'

'She's here for the audition,' Norbert cut in before Mad Cap could reply or ask why everybody seemed to be thinking her mother was 'poor'.

Norbert was sweating like nobody's business inside his rabbit costume and didn't seem to be enjoying the whole fancy-dress thing at all.

Madgie wrote her name in the notepad.

'The list is full, off you go now, chop-chop!' announced Mrs Soup to the disappointment of the few people who had joined the queue behind Mad Cap. 'Jolly good! I can go in now and finish my Scrabble Scramble prototype. Or should I call it Scramble Scrabble? Must make a note of that.'

She folded her papers, dragged the table inside and within seconds Norbert and Mad Cap were left on their own outside the front door.

'Listen,' Madgie began, 'I'm ...'

I'm what? she thought. Was she sorry? Was she still a bit cross? Was she embarrassed? What was it she had come to tell Norbert? She stared at her feet as if she would find an answer in the mud patterns on her runners. She'd never felt so awkward before.

At last, she opened her mouth. She still had no idea what she was going to say, but anything had to be better than a big fat silence.

'Hang on,' Norbert began. He had been busy tearing off the rabbit costume and was now in the process of beheading it.

Mad Cap looked up from her shoes and noticed his socks: the furry ones with little pompoms stuck on the back of the heels. Just like a rabbit's tail, she now realised.

'I'm sorry. I've been a complete eejit. It's because of this panto business. Costumes give me the creeps. I mean, not your superhero one, of course. But I don't like wearing extra heads and so on. It makes me cranky. Friends?'

As always with Norbert, things were clear and easy. *Easy as one, two, three!* Madgie thought happily.

Norbert offered his hand. Madgie shook it delightedly.

'Listen,' she said, remembering suddenly why she had come to the Soups' house in the first place. 'There's stuff going on.'

'Stuff? Surely you want to be more specific than that,' replied Norbert seriously, and for a second she thought he might go into his foul mood again.

'Well,' she said, racking her brain for a better word, 'you know … *things.*'

'Ah, I see, things!' he said with a wink and a smile. 'We're back in business then!'

Madgie had seen Norbert's bedroom many times. She had seen it during his astronomy phase, littered with blocks of cheddar carved in the shape of the moon. She had seen it covered in his sisters' colourful tights when he was trying to invent an eighth colour of the rainbow. She had seen it black with soot when he had wanted to be a chemist.

So when she stepped into the room that morning after telling Norbert everything over a cup of hot chocolate in the kitchen, she was a bit disappointed. There was a torch on the desk, a pile of bright orange flags in a corner (like the ones they wave at planes in the airport) and a mousetrap sitting in the middle of the carpet. And that was all.

'Welcome,' Norbert said grandly, 'to the Temple of Codes!'

Noticing Mad Cap wasn't as impressed as he'd hoped, he added sheepishly, 'Well, I wanted to build a bonfire to work on smoke messages, but Mum said 'no way' after the chemistry experiments. I tried with a candle, but it just wasn't the same.'

'What's that thing doing here?' asked Madgie, pointing at the mousetrap. 'Surely Scrum can do that job. Or is he too fat and lazy?'

This last bit she whispered, seeing the huge cat emerging from under the bed. Scrum rubbed against her legs, nearly sending her sprawling, and thumped his way out of the room, making Norbert's paperclip collection rattle in its jam jar.

Norbert picked up the mousetrap.

'This,' he announced 'is ... well, will soon be ... a Morse transmitter.'

'Morse?' Mad Cap repeated. 'I know him. The guy from the telly. Mum's soft on him, but Dad says it's all fanciful gobbledegook and real inspectors don't have time for crosswords.'

Norbert rolled his eyes.

'Not *that* Morse, you big eejit! *This* one,' he

said, producing a sheet full of dots and lines.

'Well,' replied Madgie, a bit huffily, 'I don't think real inspectors have time for join the dots either!'

Wisely, Norbert said nothing. Instead, he took a metal skewer and crawled under his desk. Mad Cap followed. They were a bit cramped down there, but she didn't mind. They were pals again.

'Listen,' called Norbert as he banged the skewer three times, very quickly, on the pipe that ran along the wall.

He shoved the paper into Madgie's hands and said: 'Three short signals. Like dots. That's an S. See it on the chart?'

Mad Cap's eyes brightened.

'Ah, *this* Morse!'

Norbert gave three more beats with his skewer, but this time they were further apart.

'We'll call that three long. Like the dashes,' he said. 'So what's that?'

Madgie scanned the sheet.

'O!' she cried. 'Hang on!'

She took the metal stick from her friend's

hand and whacked it three times, like he had done in the first place.

'SOS!' she shouted, delighted with herself. 'How cool is that?'

It was Norbert's turn to be a bit peeved. He was supposed to be the mastermind here. It was *his* idea and *his* bedroom and *his* skewer. He went to grab the stick again –

And that's when it happened.

They got a reply.

At first, Norbert thought Madgie was still playing with the skewer, but she was peering at the chart, working out how to Morse code 'muffin'. She looked up, curious.

'Do it again, Nor. I didn't catch …'

She stopped. The boy had turned yellow. Just like the rabbit.

'Wha –'

'Shhh!' he hissed.

There it was again. Norbert snatched the paper away from Mad Cap. That didn't make sense! He screwed up his eyes and listened.

_ · _   ··   ·_··   ·_··

He checked it again. No, he had been right

the first time. Madgie glanced at the chart over his shoulder.

'K,' she deciphered 'I-L-L. K-I-L-L? Kill what?' She checked her chart again. 'It's too long, I lost it. Was it "kill the rats"?'

'Not the rats,' Norbert answered darkly. 'The brats. It says "kill the brats".'

Mad Cap gulped. And then she flared into a rage.

'Oh yeah? Kill the brats? Well, here's what the brats have to say to that!'

She picked up the skewer again and thrashed the pipe with it like a mad hard-rock drummer. The more she banged, the more urgent the menacing message came. Faster and faster, louder and louder. Madgie was laughing now, as much from relief as anything. Norbert joined in and the din became fantastic.

Until it all ended in a long, horrifying yell that seemed to come out of the pipe.

The two friends stopped dead. They stared at each other. And made a run for it.

Scrambling out from under the desk was hard work. They were in each other's way and the skewer seemed to be poking at them of its own accord. Then they were out on the carpet, running to the door, fumbling with the knob and pushing like sumo wrestlers against the thick wooden panel.

But it wouldn't budge. Norbert threw himself on the floor and tried to see what was blocking it. He caught a glimpse of unruly ginger hair and enormous claws. Scrum. That fat door-stopper of a cat. The mini-elephant.

'We're trapped!' he yelled in panic.

6

— .... .. —. —.—

.. — —.

'Let me think,' Norbert panted. 'Just let me think.'

He was sitting on the bed, his hands pressed against his ears to block out the mad clanging from the pipe under the desk. Madgie, happy to let the genius do the thinking, was crouched in front of the door, talking sweet talk to Scrum on the other side.

Every now and then, she would make a suggestion.

'We could try the window,' she offered.

Norbert shook his head.

'Nope. Dad painted it half shut after I tried my bungee-jumping experiment.'

'How about the fireplace?'

'What fireplace?'

'Oh! Yeah.'

The banging on the pipes was still going strong but at least the shouts had stopped. Now a new voice could be heard above the noise. It was shrill and cross and coming closer. Mad Cap scurried over to the bed, and she and Norbert sat there clutching each other's arms and waiting for the worst.

Suddenly, the bedroom door crashed open. At the same time, three things happened:

1. Norbert's sister appeared with a bored-looking parrot perched on her shoulder.

2. Madgie realised that the door opened inwards and that they hadn't been trapped after all.

3. Norbert dropped dead.

Well, not really. But he went all yellow again and he squeezed Mad Cap so hard she shrieked. But no one noticed, because his sister, Gloria, was yelling, 'Stop that racket, Norbert Soup! I'm trying to teach this eejit of a bird to speak and I need … *Ouch!*'

Maybe the parrot couldn't speak, but it could obviously hear, and it didn't like being called an eejit. Its beak clamped with a vicious snap on Gloria's sister's finger and she ran down the stairs, yelling some more and calling the bird all sorts of horrible names. It learnt a lot that day.

Norbert let out a deep sigh, then he picked himself up from the bed and made for the door.

'Phew!' he said. 'For a sec, I thought it was Mrs Mudrick.'

'Norbert, this is your *bedroom!*' said Madgie. 'How come you don't know which way the door opens?'

'I was in a panic,' Norbert explained sheepishly.

'And what was that about Mrs Mudrick? What would *she* be doing here?'

'Maybe she saw you coming in. Weren't you

supposed to bring her some meat this morning?'

'Janie! I completely forgot. You're right – she *will* come after me!'

She shivered at the thought of the knitted blanket and the message on it. *Fitzmarcel Die!* She never *ever* wanted to go near that madwoman again.

'We've got to hide you,' Norbert decided. 'How about your place? That box-room with the punchball and all your dad's old Lego men?'

'No,' she said. 'He's just decided to clear it out.'

As she said this, she remembered what her mother had said when Dad had started on the box-room: 'There isn't much time left'.

Madgie felt as if she had just been hit by a runaway breeze-block or a flying Scrum. She'd have to talk to Norbert about this. He would know what was going on and what to do.

But for the moment he was clearly on to something else.

'The den!' he announced. 'Under the bridge. You can hide there for a while. Go and pack a survival kit. I'll meet you there in an hour.'

Now that her mother had swapped all the biscuits and crisps for carrot sticks and broccoli heads, there was nothing much around the kitchen that Mad Cap wanted to have in her survival kit.

Still, she was here now so she might as well pick up a few things. She stashed some organic wholegrain bread in a cotton bag (trying not to think of the sharp bits of cereal that always got stuck in her teeth), a measly looking apple which would probably be too floury and a bottle of plain, boring water.

Then she ran up to her room to grab her big woolly cardi and earmuffs, but as she was crossing the landing she heard Colm stomping out of the bathroom. She could tell he was going to give her grief over the missing diary and she really didn't have time for that.

She jumped into the laundry basket outside his bedroom door, brought the lid down on her head and stopped breathing. Not because she thought she'd be heard, but because of the stench. It was like forty badgers had invited all their friends and relatives to a cheese fondue.

Madgie was quickly running out of air in there, but she would stick it out. Colm wasn't going to take all day crossing that landing and disappearing into his room, was he?

Just then, she felt him bump into the basket and heard him fumbling with his doorknob. Another second or two and the coast would be clear.

'Hang on, young man!' came a cry from further along the landing. 'Stop those space shuttle engines of yours and come back down to Earth with me for a sec, would you?'

Great. Now Madgie's mother was there too and she'd called Colm 'young man' – this could take a while. With a sinking feeling, Mad Cap opened her mouth, emptied her lungs and filled them up again. Oh, man! This was really vile! She could almost *taste* the smell.

She groped for the bottle of water in her bag and tried to drown the disgusting stink, splashing Colm's dirty socks and underwear in the process.

'What's the story with your sister?' Mrs

Cappock continued. 'Why are you still being so mean to her?'

Mad Cap hastily put her bottle away and pricked up her ears. This could be good!

'Aw, Mum!' wailed Colm.

'Things are going to be hard enough, so in the meantime she can really do without your nonsense!'

What will be hard enough? thought Madgie. *For who? And why does EVERYONE ELSE know about this?*

'But Mum! *She nicked my diary!*' Colm exploded, machine-gunning each word as if he was fighting a bunch of space invaders. 'And I don't see why we shouldn't tell her about the other thing. She's a tough cookie, she can take it.'

'Right,' Mrs Cappock said. 'First of all, you don't *know* she stole it. With all those guards in the family, you of all people should know you can't accuse someone without proof. And I can't see your evidence. Oh, chickpea,' she added more gently, 'I'm sorry. I know how it feels.'

For a moment, Madgie wondered about

that. Mum would never keep a secret diary, would she? She'd have nothing to write about. 'Monday: planted two rows of peas and killed twenty-seven slugs.' Fascinating stuff!

Actually, she thought, Colm's diary wasn't exactly top secret either. Not like her own secret mission log. Now if someone stole *that* ... She felt a chill run down her scalp all the way to her toes. She'd have to ask Norbert for extra security tips.

'As for the other thing,' Mum was saying, 'it'll be time to tell her soon. But not till I'm good and ready, you hear? Can I trust you on that one?'

Colm must have made some sort of nod, because next thing Mad Cap heard her mum going down the stairs.

Suddenly she was sick of nobody telling her anything. And so, without wasting another second, she burst out of the laundry basket and nearly gave Colm a heart attack.

'AAAAAAARGGH!' he shouted, taking a step back and hovering dangerously near the edge of the top step.

Mad Cap was on him in two ticks, neatly

pinning him on the carpet and stopping him from breaking his neck. Those wrestling lessons had paid off after all.

'What's going on?' she hissed. 'What's wrong with Mum? Why did Manic Mudrick call her a poor thing and why does Mrs Soup hug her like there's no tomorrow and why is she always tired and is she going to die and is it my fault and ...'

Madgie didn't know how worried she was until she heard herself roll out all her questions. She probably had a few more (about why mozzarella was suddenly junk food and was it really the lemon sherbet that shrank Mum's work apron), but at that stage she was crying and crying and crying, and Colm did the weirdest thing he'd ever done in his life: he got back on his knees and pulled down her hoodie and put his arm around her neck, but gently, and ruffled her hair and kissed her on the cheek.

Mad Cap was so shocked she stopped crying instantly.

'Madgie Madonna Cappock,' Colm said, 'you are the biggest eejit on Barnaby Street, do you know that?'

She was going to protest that she wasn't an eejit and that nobody was allowed to use her middle name, ever, but he went on: 'Nobody's going to die, you silly moo! It's just that Mum's expecting a new arrival, that's all.'

'Grandma's coming to live with us?' shrieked Madgie, horrified.

'Oh man, you're thick! Not that kind of arrival! Mum's going to *have a baby!* Why do you think Dad finally cleared out the box-room? I told them the baby could have your bedroom and we could send you to the shed, but they said … Hey! Where are you going?' he shouted as his sister hared down the stairs and then, in a lower voice, 'Don't tell them I told you, OK?'

But Madgie wasn't listening. Her mind was like a washing machine, spinning at full tilt, shaking and rumbling, and a little bit foamy on top.

A new baby? What for? What would it look like? What if it's another Colm? Imagine being sandwiched between two silly, smelly boys? But if it was a girl … Maybe Grandma would pick on her instead of Madgie. That'd be good. On the other hand, maybe Mum and Dad would like her better than they liked Madgie, being all new and cute.

All these questions and more, many more, tumbled around her head as she skidded to a halt at the kitchen table. Her mother was making an abominably healthy-looking salad. Her top looked all wrong, but now Madgie knew why, and her cheeks were all red and her eyes were full of tears, but now Madgie could see they were tears of joy.

Mum opened her arms and Madgie ran into them.

'It's going to be fine, sweetpea.'

'Why didn't you *say* anything?' Madgie demanded.

'We were going to tell you everything after my next hospital appointment. They said that then they can see if all is well and they'll know if it's a boy or a girl. Maybe you'd like to come with me? To the hospital, I mean.'

Would she like that? Madgie wondered. Did she want to know anything about this 'new arrival'? She waited for her spinning brain to slow down, but it just wouldn't.

Mum put Madgie's hand on her belly and instantly she could feel a kick. Madgie moved her hand away. Her mother didn't seem to have noticed anything. Madgie touched the bulging blouse again. There it was! A little foot had just kicked her in its own Morse code.

'So, what do you think?' Mrs Cappock asked again. 'Will you come?'

One last time, Madgie pressed her hand against her mum's bump. *Kick!* That felt like a 'Yes', she thought. In fact, it felt like a 'You'd better or else …'

So Mad Cap had no choice, really.

'When are we going?' she said.

'Monday morning at eight. I can drop you to school on the way back.'

Monday at eight? Well, she'd just have to get Sapphire's food a little later, at break or lunchtime. Surely Mrs Mudrick wouldn't mind …

And then, finally, Madgie remembered that the old madwoman wanted her dead. Because who could have been sending that awful message that she and Norbert had got on the pipes earlier that morning? Someone who enjoyed knitting bloody daggers and death threats into her blankies, that was who.

Madgie had a date with Norbert at the den. It was time she got going. Her life very likely depended on it.

She kissed her mother, grabbed her survival kit and ran out of the house, her brain rattling like crazy, but to a new tune this time:

Kill the brats, kill the brats, kill the brats ...

The den under the Grand Canal Bridge was damp and miserable and Madgie had to wait ages for Norbert. To pass the time, she tried to imagine what the 'new arrival' would look like and came to the conclusion that it would probably be pink and wrinkled and bald. Not a pretty sight.

Then she wondered whether she should tell Norbert about it, but decided against it. She wasn't at all sure what he would say. He might laugh at her. Or worse, he might say, 'Well, of course, I had already guessed from such-and such a clue.'

She nearly felt cross already. Better think of something else, something funny … like Colm's face when Mum would ask him why his underwear was all wet. Sniggering, Mad Cap took out the bottle of water she had half spilled in the laundry basket.

The water felt as if it was about to freeze. Where on earth was Norbert?!

She was beginning to think that facing evil Mrs Mudrick mightn't be as painful as catching pneumonia when her friend finally arrived.

'I have a plan!' he said with a beam, taking something out of his rucksack.

It was the rabbit costume's head.

'No way!' shouted Madgie. 'I'm Mad Cap, not Fluffy Bunny.'

'Oh come on! It's just for a while. We'll put you outside the sports hall until the audition is over and then I'll take you home. I'll say I always wanted a man-sized dummy rabbit and there'll be no problem, honest! And Mudrick will *never* spot you.'

But he could tell it wasn't going to work. Mad Cap stuck her tongue out at him and that was the end of that. Anyway, the signal had said 'kill the *brats*' – more than one brat. Why did Norbert seem to think that only Mad Cap was in danger from the evil witchy woman?

'Anyway,' he said, 'the ladies' table quiz training session is on right now, and Mrs M is a member, so for the moment you're safe.'

She relaxed, but Norbert was chundering on.

'We must put Mudrick out of the picture,' he announced.

'What picture?' asked Mad Cap, unimpressed.

'There's something fishy about her. She's a knitting maniac and I'd bet my pocket-money she had something to do with Mr Fitzmarcel's disappearance.'

'And she shampoos her hair with Ribena!' added Madgie, warming to the theme. 'And her cat. Oh, man!'

She did an impersonation of Scary Sapphire and that had them in stitches for a whole ten minutes. Then Norbert took out a pen and set to work.

'What we need, really, is to prove she abducted the butcher,' he declared.

'What if she didn't, though?' objected Mad Cap.

'Hmph. Never mind that.'

They did a bit more thinking. Lunchtime came and went. Fortunately, Norbert had brought a few goodies: bacon-flavoured Hula Hoops and salt-and-vinegar peanuts. They munched on in silence.

Eventually, Madgie said, 'It's funny, I got two missions in one week and they were both to go and get something from the butcher's shop.'

'What's funny about that?' asked Norbert.

'Well, Mum and Mrs Mudrick didn't really need Rent-a-Hero to do their shopping, did they? But Mr Fitzmarcel, he needs us – you know, to rescue him. Except he's not around to hire us. That's kind of funny. And so I thought ...'

'It's not funny,' Norbert interrupted her. 'The technical term is *paradoxical*.'

Madgie stared at him as if he had donkey ears sticking out of his head.

'What's wrong with you?' Norbert said defensively. 'That word got me a heap of points in the Junior Scrabble tournament, I might as well use it!'

Mad Cap just shook her head. Junior Scrabble tournament? Then again, she was thinking about joining the big origami marathon next Christmas, so she couldn't really judge.

'Anyway,' she said. 'I was thinking we could hire *ourselves* to rescue Mr Fitzmarcel. Would that be funny? Or paradoc-thingy?'

At this, Norbert's eyes almost popped out of his head. He sat up so suddenly he nearly banged his head against the roof of the bridge. To avoid the hard brick he took a step forward – and put a foot in the cold canal water. He was so excited, he didn't even notice.

'Of course!' he said.

'Of course what?' asked Madgie, smirking at the sight of the sodden pompom sock. (Did he never change his socks? she wondered. Or did he just have a whole stash of matching ones?)

'*That's* what we have to do,' said Norbert. 'We have to find Mr Fitzmarcel, prove Manic Mudrick is as guilty as the cat who stole the cream and then you'll be safe!'

'*I* will? We *both* will! "Brats" includes you too.'

Norbert ignored that.

'Mad Cap,' he concluded, 'you're a genius. And that's a technical term.'

DEAD BODIES AND STUFF

Mad Cap was chuffed. Being called a genius by a genius – you couldn't beat that. But at the same time, she wasn't quite sure she deserved it. She had just been thinking aloud, really. She hadn't been trying to come up with a brilliant idea and a brilliant plan, like Norbert did. Maybe he was just being nice.

But nice or not, the boy was in full Cluedo mode now.

'We have a suspect, but no weapon yet,' he said. 'As for the crime scene, I can think of two places. Mrs Mudrick's house …'

Madgie winced. She wasn't going back there. But he could be right. The place stank. There could *easily* be a dead body in that dump.

'Or the butcher's shop,' Norbert finished. 'There's bound to be tons of clues in there.'

'Yeah!' Mad Cap replied. 'Maybe we'll find dead bodies in the cold-room!'

'Course we will.'

Madgie stared at her friend. She'd been joking about the dead bodies.

'We will?'

'Sure! Dead cows and pigs and stuff, you big eejit! What do you think a cold-room is *for*? Come on, let's do some thinking. Or else … chop-chop!'

Madgie rolled her eyes. She was pretty sure Norbert was only joking and nobody was going to get their head chopped off. But just in case, she wrinkled her brow and scratched her chin and really did do some thinking.

Some time later, after plans A, B, C and C+ had been drafted, rejected, fine-tuned and finally voted on; after Norbert had drilled every last detail of it into Madgie's head; after he had checked and repacked the survival kit several times, the Rent-a-Hero team entered the butcher's shop. Madgie was in the lead, crouching low under the counter, and Norbert brought up the rear, ready to deliver the first line of his script.

''llo,' croaked the plumber, who was standing in for the butcher. She was juggling with three pairs of pliers and a bare T-bone. 'You want?'

Norbert cleared his throat. If he wanted to capture the woman's attention while Mad Cap did her bit of snooping around, he had to get this right. He had to ask her for something tricky – and he thought he knew just what.

'A slice of ham, please,' he said in the loud, clear voice he used to recite poems in school.

The butcher-plumber's face fell, and with it the pliers and the T-bone.

'Egad!' she muttered as she turned to the counter.

She picked up several pieces of meat, one by one, and poked at them in turn, and put her ear to each one, as if she thought it was going to tell her its name. While she went through the sausages, Norbert gave Mad Cap a nudge. It was time to go.

Madgie didn't hesitate. She darted through the door at the back of the shop and within a second she was out of sight.

'Got ya!' cried Mrs Fitzmarcel and for a horrible moment, Norbert thought she had spotted Mad Cap.

But no. She was brandishing a chicken breast and waving it at the boy.

'There's your ham. That all?'

Norbert was about to answer when it all went awfully, terribly, disastrously WRONG. As she turned to the till, Mrs Fitzmarcel noticed the open door. She went very pale, dropped the meat and in two steps was at the door. She banged it shut with Madgie still inside. And unless Norbert was very much mistaken, it was the butcher's cold-room that Mad Cap had got herself trapped in.

The woman picked up the chicken from the floor, dumped it in a bag with trembling fingers and asked, 'Anything else I can do for you?'

Norbert couldn't take his eyes off the door. It was very closed.

'No,' he answered in a daze, taking the bag from Mrs Fitzmarcel. 'No, thanks. That's quite enough.'

The room was darker than Colm's sock drawer and about as smelly. Madgie could see absolutely nothing – nothing except a faint white mist just in front of her.

'A ghost!' she gasped. And the mist got stronger.

She stumbled backwards, almost banging against the door. But her survival kit on her back had cushioned the shock.

Meanwhile, the mist was still there. Coming and going like clockwork. Mad Cap's teeth were chattering so hard she thought they were doing Morse code.

'It's flipping cold in here!' she moaned.

Then she got it. The cold-room! She was trapped in the rotten cold-room! And that misty ghost was only the icy breath coming out of her own mouth.

She hadn't *really* believed it was a ghost anyway. Ghosts normally don't smell of bacon Hula Hoops.

Shuddering with the cold, she got her rucksack off her back, but instead of her survival kit, she found she had somehow got hold of Norbert's bag.

'Janie!' she muttered. 'How did that happen?'

So much for all that careful repacking. She rummaged in the backpack and pulled out the yellow rabbit suit. It wasn't exactly comfy when she put it on over her clothes, but at least it was warm.

Some superhero, she thought. *And I have this smashing cape and mask and stuff at home! Missions never go according to plan, even when you have a genius on the team. Or two, for that matter. It's just like they say on the pack of sugar at Grandma's: 'Life is full of surprises.'*

And of course, talking of surprises, there was

the baby business to think about, too. Madgie counted on her rabbit fingers. There would be ten years between her and the 'new arrival', which meant that when it turned ten, Madgie would be … older than Colm was now! She hoped she wouldn't be half as annoying. What would it be like being the *older* sister for a change? Would she be bossy? Would she be proud? Would she show the little one the den? Would she have to change a nappy? Eeek!

Madgie could hear her brain going into high-spin mode again. She pressed her rabbit paws against her forehead.

Her head cleared.

'Now,' she announced to the dark shapes she could just about make out. 'I've got a mission. Let's go!'

She pricked up her rabbit ears and gave a good listen. Nothing. She was on her own.

Or was she? She thought she could hear some sort of knocking now, coming from somewhere beyond the cold-room. As she made for the sound, she had to slalom between huge shadowy masses that hung before her in the cold air.

The noise was clearer, nearer now, but she could tell it was still some way away. She kept going towards it.

_ · _ ·· ·_·· ·_··

While she paused to think where she had heard this rhythm before, she leaned against the wall.

'I know this code! If only ... Oh no! It's ...'

The wall she was leaning against suddenly swung away from her and she landed on her rabbit bum. The wall came swinging back and dropped down on top of her.

Ouch! It wasn't a wall, then ... It was a dead body.

But that was not as frightening as it seemed, she told herself hurriedly, because, as Norbert had pointed out, that's what you get in cold-rooms. Dead bodies. Of sheep and cows and stuff. Right?

Suddenly she wasn't so sure.

The cold meat muffled her scream.

Norbert sat speechless on the kerb outside the butcher's and tried to think.

He had no idea how to get Mad Cap out of there. If she was stuck in that cold-room …

He was about to go back inside and tell everything to Mrs Fitzmarcel when he heard the shop's metal shutters coming down with a furious racket.

What could he do about Madgie now? He quickly ran through his options.

1. He could go to their parents and confess everything. But he couldn't really, because it would be the end of Rent-a-Hero if anybody found out about their snooping around people's shops and houses.

2. He could go to the police. But see 1.

Or

3. He could just go on.

Mad Cap was well capable of looking after herself. Wasn't she? Surely she would find a window or something and get out of there as fast as she could. They'd meet at the den later and have a laugh.

Norbert considered option 3 again. He *could*

go on. Because there was a plan D that came after C+. And that was to investigate their prime suspect: Manic Mudrick.

He glanced at the time on his multi-task digiwatch. He'd have to be quick. The audition for the panto was due to start in about an hour and he had promised his mother he'd be there in his rabbit costume to try to get the main part. How exactly she had made him promise that, he wasn't quite sure now.

He took a deep breath, got up and made his way towards Mrs Mudrick's house.

Madgie scrambled frantically under the sheep's corpse. Retching and panting, she eventually managed to roll it off to one side. Her heart in her mouth, she stood up again and ran as hard as she could.

As she ran, she tried not to think. She knew the cold-room was full of dead animals, but there was every chance that one of these dead things was Mr Fitzmarcel. Where else would you hide a dead body if you were a butcher's evil wife who preferred plumbing tools to meat (Mrs Fitzmarcel) or a butcher's evil neighbour with a *definite wish* for the death of said butcher (Mrs Mudrick)?

Was she (whichever 'she' it might be) planning to feed poor Mr Fitzmarcel to people? Or to cats?

Then Mad Cap heard the knocking again. In her fright, she had forgotten where she knew that sound from, and she decided to follow it.

There was a thin crack of light behind what seemed to be a huge ham. Gingerly, Madgie tiptoed around the ham and – oh, yay! – there was a door. She ran her fingers along the door frame and found a switch.

The cold-room light came on with a series of flickerings that went on and on and on. The bulb must be faulty, thought Mad Cap, blinking like a mole on a sunbed. Then it hit her: this was the flashing she had seen from Colm's bedroom window. Someone had been in this cold-room in the middle of the night. They hadn't been signalling to her. They'd just turned on the stupid neon and it had blinked on and off for ages.

What were the Fitzmarcels *doing* in here at midnight when honest people were snoring in their beds (or, let's face it, stealing their brothers' diaries)?

Mad Cap tightened her rabbit costume around her.

She opened the door out of the cold-room and saw a dusty staircase ahead, lined with bricks and cobwebs and plunging into what must be a basement. The sound was coming from there, so Madgie followed it carefully.

Now she could hear some sort of music as well as the tapping, like a hundred shivering penguins playing the violin. It could have been in a horror movie. One with madwomen stabbing innocent people in the shower, Madgie reckoned.

'Let's finish this!' she announced to the unknown. 'Mad Cap forever and beyond!'

She went on creeping carefully down the stairs. Finally, she came to another door. She pushed, and it opened with a creak. In the room beyond was the most horrible thing Madgie M. Cappock had ever seen in her life.

She *screamed*.

SAPPHIRE AND THE MAGIC SPUDS

Mrs Mudrick's front garden looked like a minefield. Mould was licking at the door step and, worst of all, the old net curtains in the front window had cats embroidered on them. Norbert shuddered.

This time, the sign on the door said:

IF YOU CAN READ THIS,
YOU'RE ALREADY TOO CLOSE.

Of course the door was locked. As Norbert walked around to the back, he thought he saw a movement at the window. The curtains had twitched, he was sure of it. Pretty sure …

The back garden wasn't in much better condition than the front. A forest of mutant dandelions with stems as thick as tree trunks was eating away at the patio. Wooden crates marked 'Top Quality Wool' were piled high against the crumbling shed, probably holding it upright. But on the back door, Norbert found what he was looking for.

'Bingo!'

He rummaged in one of the crates until he found a piece of wool long enough, tied a stone at one end, then went back to the door. It had no knob on the outside, but it had a cat flap. Norbert pushed the flap inwards and plunged his hand inside and up. With one lucky flick, he managed to lasso the string around the handle.

'Ouch!'

Someone – something – had grabbed his wrist. Someone or something with claws and sharp teeth. And possibly called Sapphire.

'Oy! Let go!'

But Sapphire wasn't letting go. She bit and scratched and hissed until Norbert had to remove his arm if he ever wanted to play air guitar again.

While he nursed his injured hand, he could hear the cat having a go at the string inside the door.

There was a sudden click. The cat's playful pouncing on the wool had managed to unlock the door from the inside, even though Norbert hadn't been able to do it. But he'd been the genius who'd thought of the plan, so that was fine.

'Yes!' he cried and threw himself at the door. He tumbled into the kitchen, but immediately leapt to his feet again in case Sapphire was planning another attack.

She wasn't, though. She had got completely tangled up in the wool.

Norbert sighed with relief. That was one less problem. But when he breathed in again he nearly gagged.

'Holy Mildred! It pongs in here! Did *you* do that?' he asked Sapphire.

The cat gave him such an innocent look that for a second he thought, *What a nice little kitty!* But the next moment, the piece of wool broke. Sapphire landed on the grimy tiles with a bump, struggled free from the wool and rushed at Norbert.

There was nothing he could do. He fell over, dropping his shopping bag as he did so. The bag! The cat made a beeline for it. She ripped it open, sniffed at the chicken breast inside and let out a terrifying screech.

Norbert simply couldn't move. He stared, amazed and scared to bits, as Sapphire, instead of tucking into the juicy meat, picked it up and carried it to a dark corner of the kitchen where a heap of potatoes were rotting away.

She rummaged around the spuds for a while ... and then she disappeared.

'What?!'

Norbert was up again. He ran to the pile of spuds. Here, the smell was even worse. Like loo perfume mixed with old mince. One hand on his nose, he started pulling the potatoes aside. Where was this cat? It was impossible!

A few kilos of gone-off potatoes later, sweating and panting, he unearthed Sapphire's hidey-hole – and, on the ground, he spied the edge of what must be a trap-door.

Ignoring the cat, who he could now see hidden behind more potatoes piled high in the corner and who was doing something awful to the chicken breast, he shovelled through the spuds again until the spot was clear. They were getting heavier and heavier, and the work was tiring, but there was no doubt about it. It definitely was a trap-door.

He knelt down and opened the panel.

'Stainless steel,' he muttered. 'Perfectly oiled. Hmmm.'

It's light enough even for an oldie like Mrs Mudrick to lift easily, he thought. *But how does she manage to move the spuds to get at it? She must be in training.* He hadn't reckoned that knitting was so physical.

He pinched his nose and went down through the trap-door.

At first, Norbert thought he had stepped into a badly run graveyard. It reeked of dead bodies and was pitch black except for the faint light coming from the kitchen above him. He just had time to catch a glimpse of stairs going down and a mountain of meat abandoned by Sapphire – *this cat* must *be a hoarder*! he thought – before the trap-door shut with a deafening bang over his head and he was plunged into darkness. Very smelly darkness.

Then came another noise. *Click, click, click.*

Norbert checked but it wasn't his teeth chattering, or his knees. He was too scared even for that. He pricked up his ears. *Click, click – click, click – meow.* It was Sapphire, clicking her claws on the concrete steps. She must have followed him inside and now he was trapped in a hellish hole with a mad cat who stored her excess meat underground!

He listened again. The *click-click* was more distant and the meowing more insistent.

'I see,' muttered Norbert, feeling sick. 'She wants me to follow her down the stairs.'

And because there was nothing else he could do, he did.

He went deeper and deeper into the bowels of the Earth, slowly at first, and then at rocket speed when he tripped on the cat and went rolling and rolling. He landed with a crash and an ouch and a meow and gingerly got off poor Sapphire.

It took a while for Norbert's brain to stop spinning inside his skull.

'I can see fairies! This is *not* good ...'

There was a little glowing dot of light in front of him. Norbert put his hand up to it and pushed. *Light!*

A bright neon tube lit up above his head. So much for the fairies. It was only a light switch.

Sapphire flicked her tail as if to say, *I told you it was fine down here,* and trotted deeper into the basement of Mrs Mudrick's house.

Again, Norbert, half-blinded and covered in bruises, followed. He had to bend a few times to avoid leaky pipes and he had no idea where he was going. Not to mention that it was nearly time for the flipping panto audition and his bunny act!

Maybe it was because he had just been thinking about the rabbit thing. Maybe it was because he had gone gaga. Or maybe it was real. But when he pushed the steel door at the end of the corridor and heard a horrible yell, he could have sworn it was a fluffy yellow bunny that was screaming.

KILL THE BRATS

Mr Fitzmarcel had never had bad hair days. Because Mr Fitzmarcel had never had hair, good or bad. So it took Madgie a while to recognise him with his wig on. And his tutu.

This was the terrible sight that made her screech when she opened the door in the basement under the butcher's shop, at precisely the same moment that Norbert opened the door that led from Mrs Mudrick's basement into Mr Fitzmarcel's.

Mrs Mudrick, however, recognised Mad Cap instantly, bunny costume or not.

'That evil brat again!' she shrieked.

She was standing behind the butcher, a knitting needle in one hand, beating the rhythm on an old pipe. _ . _ .. ._.. ._..

'Oh, Clotworthy!' she wailed. 'Our secret has been found out! We're doomed!'

She made as if to stab herself with the needle. Madgie stared, motionless, as the big butcher (Clotworthy?!) ran to her with a weird clickety-clack. He seized the needle and threw it away, knocking the bare lightbulb sideways. In the moving light, Mad Cap noticed all at once that the butcher was wearing tap dancing shoes, that Sapphire was nibbling heartily at his calves and that *Norbert* (how had *he* got here?) had just arrived in the room, his hands clapped over his ears.

At last, she realised she was still bawling.

She stopped.

'Wow!' said Norbert, once he had tiptoed around the adults and joined Mad Cap. 'If it doesn't work out for you as a superhero, you can always apply for a job as an ambulance siren!'

He blinked.

'Nice outfit!' he added.

'Oh, Norbert, you'll never believe it,' Mad Cap spluttered. 'I was in the cold-room and the light was the exact same light I saw before and there was a door hidden behind a dead body and then some stairs and then a basement and then a rabbit and then –'

'And then I think I can see for myself,' Norbert cut in. 'In case you hadn't noticed, I'm here too.'

What he could also see, in his mind's eye at least, was how the two houses must be sharing the same basement, how they must be interconnected. A very clear map of the buildings was taking shape in his head, but he could tell this wasn't the time for a lecture on the quaint architecture of Barnaby Street. By now, Mr Fitzmarcel had clobbered Sapphire over the head and Mrs Mudrick was petting the dazed cat between her wrinkly arms. Together, they turned on Mad Cap and Norbert, a mean, bad, ugly look in their eyes. Or actually, two mean, bad ugly looks, one on each of their nasty faces.

'So, you've discovered our little secret, then?' snarled the butcher.

'No, what do you mean?' said Madgie, as if she hadn't noticed that Mr Fitzmarcel was wearing a wig and a tutu. She was wearing a bright yellow bunny costume herself – who was she to talk?

Or maybe that wasn't the secret after all.

'Clotworthy isn't such an unusual name,' she said reassuringly. 'No reason to keep it a secret, really. Look at Norbert, he's very brave about *his* name.'

Norbert kicked her on the shin.

'Thanks for that,' he hissed. 'Madgie *Madonna*.'

'Don't play the innocent with me, lass,' Mr Fitzmarcel was saying. 'You've seen it all. Yes!' he shouted. 'Yes! I never really wanted to be a butcher! I always wanted to be a tap dancer! I've been practising down here *for days*. The leading role in the panto should be mine, MINE, MIIIIIIIIIIIIIIIIIIIIIIIIIIIIIIIIIIIIIIIIIINE!!!'

Mad Cap and Norbert each took a step back and managed to wedge themselves stuck in the doorway. Meanwhile, Mrs Mudrick had picked up the knitting needle and was advancing towards the broad back of the tutu-ed Fitzmarcel.

'Mind!' Norbert screamed. 'Look out behind you!'

'You think I'm going to fall for that one?' snarled Mr Fitzmarcel. 'Pah!'

Madgie gulped. 'Mad Mudrick's gonna kill you!' she shouted. 'She's coming at you with a knitting needle!'

There was a pause.

Then Fitzmarcel began to chuckle. Soon, he was laughing his wig off, and there was also a worrying noise like one of the pipes was about to burst. It took them a minute to realise that the burst-pipe-type noise was Mrs Mudrick's laughter.

'Why would such a fine woman as herself want to do me in? She's the one who's been helping me all week to rehearse for the audition, the one who shared my secret all along,' he panted, wiping away a few laughter tears.

'But she was nasty to you in the shop,' Norbert argued. 'You had such a row, she couldn't even go in there any more. Mad Cap

– I mean, Madgie – has had to do her meat shopping for her all week.'

'Oh, that was all just a cover-up,' Mrs Mudrick explained. 'A subterfuge! People still remember, you know. The Glamorous Gisella and her Ballet Flotilla! That's *me*, see?'

For a moment the not-so-glamorous Gisella was lost in the mists of her youth. Madgie tried to picture it, but all she could come up with were black and white images of a wrinkled lady wearing a leotard and comfy slippers.

She shook her head. None of this made a whole lot of sense. But at least Mr Fitzmarcel was not dead and hanging up in the cold-room, waiting to be carved into rashers. That was something. Wasn't it?

'And if the nasty gossips of Barnaby Street guessed that Clotworthy and I shared a passion for dancing …' Mrs Mudrick tailed off.

Mr Fitzmarcel shuddered. Madgie wasn't quite sure what was wrong with a dancing butcher, but she had heard the gossips before (Mrs M was one of them) and she could see why you wouldn't want to catch their attention.

'If people thought I was helping dear Clotworthy with his dancing,' Mrs Mudrick went on, 'they might think … well, they might think *anything*. And then he might not get the part in the pantomime, see? People are so *envious*, you wouldn't believe it. It's because of the panto that we have been training so hard. The night-time practice wasn't enough any more. We needed to rehearse during the day, too. That's why Clotworthy had to leave the shop to that plumber creature and I had to get Madgie to buy my Sapphire's meat for me. It was a mistake, I know now. You horrible little …'

The night-time practice! That explained why the cold-room light flickered in the night. Fitzmarcel had been sneaking down to the basement late at night to practise his tap-dancing and he'd had to go through the cold-room to get there.

But Mad Cap had had enough. She knew Mrs Mudrick was lying through her dentures. And she could prove it.

'Don't believe her!' she yelled at the butcher. 'I saw her blanket! It said "Fitzmarcel die!"

She knitted it herself. She must want you dead *very* badly.'

At that, the butcher became very serious and turned to the old woman, who was scratching her ear with the needle.

'What's that, Gisella?'

Mrs Mudrick's face turned as purple as her hair.

'You! You rotten kids! You've been nosing around where you had no business to be! If you'd stuck to the rules, none of this would be happening.'

Mr Fitzmarcel plucked the needle out of her ear and pointed it at her.

'Gisella, what's going on? Why did you want to stab me?'

'I didn't! Never!' she swore.

'But what about the blanket with that awful message in it? What is it anyway? A curse? A spell?'

Gisella Mudrick shuffled sheepishly.

'A wish,' she breathed. 'But I didn't mean *you*.'

'How many other Fitzmarcels do you know, lass?!'

She went from purple to pink as Mad Cap answered thoughtfully, 'Well, there's your wife, for one.'

The butcher faced her again. 'What wife?' he asked.

He seemed genuinely puzzled. Could he possibly have forgotten the plumber woman who, at this very moment, was probably upstairs mixing up bacon and chicken nuggets?

There was a silence. Mad Cap's mind raced. Had the man killed poor Mrs Fitz? Could he have had time in the few minutes between Mad Cap's encounter with a sheep in the cold-room and the moment she and Norbert had discovered the dancing pair? No, she decided, that was impossible.

So, in that case, there was only one question: who was the woman in the shop, the one who called herself Mrs Fitzmarcel?

Madgie braced herself and asked the question.

'She *doesn't* call herself Mrs Fitzmarcel,' said Mr Fitzmarcel.

'*Everyone* calls her Mrs Fitzmarcel,' argued Norbert.

'Do they?' asked the butcher. 'I can't say I've noticed. But anyway, that's not her name. She is in fact *Miss* Fitzmarcel. She's my sister. I'm not married. But what she's called is not very important. What I'd like to know is why would you want to kill my sister, Gisella?'

'Your ... *sister?*' repeated the old woman, flabbergasted. 'But I thought she was your ...'

The butcher scowled at her, but just then Mrs Mudrick spoke again.

'Wobbly cow! So you're *single?*'

She dropped on one old knee with a plonk and said, 'Clotworthy, I have loved thee ever since I clapped eyes on thee. Wilt thou marry me?'

The butcher nearly swallowed the knitting needle, which he had been using as a toothpick. He coughed and spluttered and retched. Mrs Mudrick took this as a yes and kissed him ferociously. (She also kissed the needle, but she didn't seem to mind.)

Norbert and Madgie closed their eyes. They had seen enough for one day.

And so, Mr Fitz and Mrs M got married and had loads of kids.

Well, no, not quite. They didn't get married straight away. First they kissed, and then they kissed again. And then when they stopped, Mr Fitzmarcel said he had loved Mrs Mudrick ever since he'd arrived in Barnaby Street a few weeks ago, but he had been too shy to tell her, and yes, of course, he loved darling little Sapphire too, and no, he didn't mean it when he called her sausage meat. And so on and so forth, so that eventually Norbert had to clear his throat and ask them could they please help him and Mad Cap out of the doorway because he, for one, had to be at the audition for the panto in about five minutes.

'Five minutes?! Chicken's bladder! I've got to go too!' cried the butcher.

He ran around the room like a headless ham, pulling a jacket and dungarees on over his tutu.

'You think they'll recognise me?' he asked his sweetheart anxiously.

'Your own mother wouldn't recognise you,' she said, tugging at Mad Cap's bunny arm. 'And if they do, and they have a problem with it, they will have me to reckon with.'

With another tug, Madgie and Norbert popped out of the doorway and were rolling on the floor.

'So nobody wants to kill us any more?' Mad Cap said in a loud whisper.

'Shhh!' hissed her friend as he picked himself up. 'Don't be giving them ideas!'

'What do you mean *kill you*?' asked the butcher. 'Where did you get such a silly notion from?'

'Silly?' mused Mrs M. 'It has some appeal ... They know our secret now.'

'But we didn't this morning when you Morse coded your death threat over to us,' Norbert pointed out.

The blank looks on Mrs Mudrick's and Mr Fitzmarcel's faces were enough to tell him they had no idea what he was talking about. Madgie picked up on it too and started clicking her tongue to the rhythm of K-I-L-L-T-H-E-B-R-

A-T-S, while Norbert translated letter by letter. Suddenly, the butcher's feet sprang into motion, tapping exactly the dots and the dashes and soon the old biddy was knocking the knitting needle against a pipe in the exact same tempo.

It was the Rent-a-Hero team's turn to look baffled.

'What was that about?' asked Madgie when Mr Fitz finally stopped.

'That,' he said, wiping a sweaty brow, 'was my very difficult and very amazing routine for the panto audition.'

'And what is she doing banging that pipe?' asked Norbert pointing at Mrs Mudrick.

'I'm helping of course! Keeping the rhythm: Stomp flap [pause] back-flap [pause] tap stomp back-flap [pause] tap stomp back-flap. They're the dance steps, you ignorant child.'

'Yes, but it's also KILL in Morse code,' countered Norbert. 'So you mean you weren't signalling to us?'

'No. But I wish we had been. Might have kept you away,' muttered the woman. 'I thought we were safe down here. I had no idea anybody could hear us.'

Norbert put his genius brain to work. It took him less than a second to figure it out.

'It's the pipes,' he said. 'This one must run into our own basement – we're only next door after all – and up through our kitchen and on to my bedroom. Fascinating …'

It was certainly very interesting (well, sort of), but Madgie was getting all sweaty in her bunny costume and she really wanted to get back to the fresh air now.

'Great!' she concluded. 'Now that we know you didn't mean to kill us and you're really lovely people, how about we leave you to it and go home?'

The butcher didn't seem convinced. 'What will we do with them?' he whispered to his sweetheart. The future *real* Mrs Fitzmarcel considered this.

'Well, I'm sure they won't tell anybody about what they've seen today, will they?'

The Rent-a-Hero team shook their heads vigorously. Even if they did tell, Norbert thought, nobody would believe a word of it and they'd probably be sent to the madhouse straight away.

'Because if they do,' continued the old woman, 'I'll feed them to Sapphire.'

Mad Cap looked horrified. Norbert looked even more horrified, because he had seen what that psycho cat had done to the innocent chicken breast.

'Grand so,' concluded Mr Fitzmarcel. 'On we go. Does the bunny need a lift?'

And so they all trooped out of the basement through Mrs Mudrick's kitchen. She tutted at the sight of the scattered potatoes. She pressed a button marked 'Spud Magnet'. All the potatoes began to buzz and zoom on the floor all the way to the trap-door.

Norbert was impressed, but there was no time to marvel. They had to move on and he still had to put on the rabbit costume. Unless …

Mad Cap still couldn't believe it. But there she was, on stage, in front of a dozen good citizens of Barnaby Street. In a bunny suit.

The mask made her nose itchy but she knew she couldn't take it off. For one thing, she'd rather spend the weekend at her grandmother's than be recognised doing an audition for a silly panto. Plus she had promised Norbert.

It was a simple deal really. Norbert's mum would think he was on stage and she would be happy. Norbert would never have to wear the stupid costume ever again – there was no way Madgie was going to get the role – and he would be happy. Madgie would look like an awful eejit, but no one would ever know and then, in exchange for all that, her friend would, at last, tell her the name he had found in Colm's diary.

Colm's girlfriend's name: this was the kind of thing a sister needed to know. It could come in very useful for blackmailing purposes.

So on she tapped across the wobbly stage, dancing along to the wobbly music and … into an open trap-door.

'Jaaaaaaaaaaaanie!' she shouted as she went through.

The jury gave her a standing ovation.

10

MAD CAP FOREVER AND BEYOND!

They say a rabbit's foot brings good luck. Mad Cap didn't know about that. If it hadn't been for that rotten costume, she probably would never have broken her leg and she probably would never have spent the night in the hospital. But then again, she would never have gotten the role either.

Not that she would take it, she thought, as she strapped herself into her wheelchair. She wouldn't recover in time. Nope, Norbert would have to do it. And that had certainly never been part of any of his plans.

She chuckled to herself while Mum installed the ramp to wheel her into the van and Colm locked the house. They were on their way to the hospital again. This time, to the maternity unit.

'What are you laughing at?' called a voice acidic as vinegar.

Madgie looked up to find Mrs Mudrick standing outside their gate. She was wearing her Sunday best and was carrying a bulging bag sporting the words 'Fitzmarcel's: Tender Loving Care for all Your Meat Needs'.

'The butcher's shop has reopened,' the old woman announced rather needlessly.

'Yes, we know,' said Madgie's mum politely.

She couldn't see why Mrs Mudrick (who didn't like anybody but her cat and would only give you the wrong time of day) had stopped by their house for a chat.

Has Mrs Mudrick become nice? Mad Cap wondered. It would be a miracle, but come to think of it, Madgie had seen far stranger things in the last forty-eight hours. If you could be a butcher and an amazing tap-dancer, if you could be a teenage rebel and a perfectionist chef with a filthy bedroom, if you could be a genius with a mission and a plan and still be a hero when the plan went out the window, well then, why couldn't an old meanie turn all smiles and sweetness?

Then again, as Madgie mulled over this transformation, she looked at the way Mrs M was wringing her hands and playing with her brand new ring, and she started to guess what all the politeness was about.

'We're engaged,' Mrs Mudrick announced. 'Clotworthy and I, I mean.'

And then Madgie understood why she was here. This couldn't be happening. Life was just a bit too full of surprises these days. She tried not to hear what came next. She tried to pretend it was all a nightmare. But Mrs M walked right up to her and (yuk!) ruffled her hair with her pointy nails and said, 'We'll be needing a bridesmaid.'

'No way. *Niet. Nein.* Poo!' Mad Cap shouted as Colm pushed her up the ramp and into the van. 'I'll never be a bridesmaid!' she yelled as they closed the door on her.

She started banging against the side of the van.

—· ——— ·—— ·— —·——

—· ——— ·—— ·— —·——

—· ——— ·—— ·— —·——

By the time they got to the hospital, her fist was nearly as painful as her broken leg.

'Madgie, stop!' her mum shouted from the front seat. 'We'll talk about this after my appointment, OK? But don't you think it would be an exciting mission for Mad Cap? It would take a hero to pull it off. And who else is going to do it?'

Madgie said nothing. She knew better now than to sniff at a mission. But still, what could be exciting or heroic about wearing a stupid dress and getting her hair done all funny and stumbling around in little heels for an entire day?

She grumbled quietly as she was wheeled out of the van, through the maternity wing and into the lift to the scans department. She grumbled still when Mum left her and Colm in the waiting room and disappeared with a couple of nurses.

She only stopped grumbling when her brother took out a marker and started drawing on her cast.

Since she'd got Norbert to sneak the diary back into Colm's room the day before, Colm had been in a far better mood. He had even promised to cook her favourite dish tonight: popcorn soup.

'What's he saying?' she asked, pointing at the cartoony creature on her shin.

'She,' Colm corrected her. 'It's you, you big eejit!'

And so it was, kind of. It had a cape and a mask and rabbit ears, and was yelling 'Mad Cap Forever and Beyond!'

Madgie was chuffed. This was the best ad for Rent-a-Hero. Not for the first time, she felt a tweak of guilt about the whole diary thing. She was about to confess everything, but then she wasn't sure a busy hospital corridor was the best place for it.

After a few minutes Mrs Cappock came back, escorted by a man in scrubs whose name, according to his badge, was Ian.

'So, what's it going to be?' Colm asked, pointing at his mum's belly.

Before Mrs Cappock could say anything, Ian answered: 'You're going to have a little brother!'

'Are you sure?' Madgie asked.

'Sure as eggs,' Ian said to her. 'I'm quite a pro, young man.'

There was a moment of silence where the Cappock family all wondered if they should tell the nurse that Madgie was not, in fact, a 'young man'. But then they all said at the same time, 'We'll see.'

'We'll keep it anyway.'

'Life's full of surprises.'

As the van trundled up the avenue, Madgie imagined a gigantic toddler whirlwinding through her bedroom, making a mess of her homework and turning her origami circus into microscopic confetti while she scooted around like a headless rabbit shouting totally useless orders and putting up totally useless barricades. For a moment, Madgie felt just that: useless, hopeless, clueless.

But then her eyes fell on the Mad Cap cartoon on her cast and she began to smile. There was no point worrying now. And when the little monster came along, Madgie would be ready. Or maybe she wouldn't, but she knew she'd be fine. She'd stitch together a *one, two, three* plan like Norbert or she'd just improvise. But she would cope. She wasn't a superhero for nothing.

Madgie stretched in her wheelchair and closed her eyes. She said it again. *Life's full of surprises.* And she felt really, really good about it.

A PAGE FROM MAD CAP'S MISSION LOG

Stuff I can Morse code by heart:

... ___ ... SOS

_ ._ .. ._.. ._.. kill

_ ..... the

_... ._. ._ _ ... brats

__ .._ .._.. ._.. _. muffin

_. ___ .___ _ _._. no way

_._. ___ ._.. __ Colm

._.. ___ ._ ... _. loves

_. ._ _ _._. ...._ _..

(That one's a secret so you'll have to work that out for yourself.)

STUFF I CAN MORSE CODE WHILE DOING TAP DANCING.

Stomp, flap [pause] back-flap [pause] tap stomp
back-flap [pause] tap stomp back-flap = KILL

Stomp [pause] heel heel heel heel [pause] toe = THE

I haven't learnt BRATS yet, it's got too many letters.
Plus Mr Fitzmarcel says there are other ways to tap it
but that's the way he does it and it's very hard and he had
a rotten time learning it and that's why he didn't like it
when we banged on the pipe in Nor's room, cause it got
him all confused and stuff. So that's the way I have to
learn it. For the wedding …

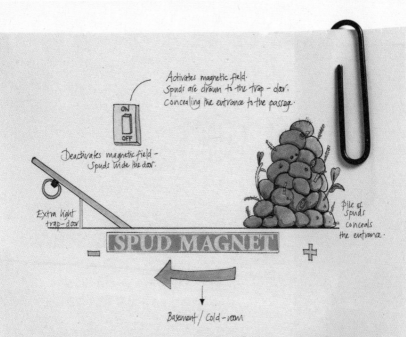

Activates magnetic field.
Spuds are drawn to the trap-door,
concealing the entrance to the passage.

Deactivates magnetic field -
Spuds slide the door.

Extra light
trap-door

SPUD MAGNET

Pile of
spuds
conceals
the entrance.

Basement / Cold-room

THE SPUD MAGNET AS OBSERVED, UNDERSTOOD AND IMPROVED BY NORBERT SOUP

When the power is on, the fake spuds and the trap-door are magnetised. The spuds (magnet +) are attracted to the trap-door (magnet -) and then the door is blocked and hidden. There is a Spud Magnet Switch on both sides of the door so you can put the spuds back into place even if you're inside, and no one will ever know.

To remove the spuds, turn the power off. Or else they're flipping heavy to lift!

NB: Baby spuds not recommended, except for very small trap-doors.

MORSE CODE

a	.—	n	—.
b	—...	o	———
c	—.—.	p	.——.
d	—..	q	——.—
e	.	r	.—.
f	..—.	s	...
g	——.	t	—
h	....	u	..—
i	..	v	...—
j	.———	w	.——
k	—.—	x	—..—
l	.—..	y	—.——
m	——	z	——..